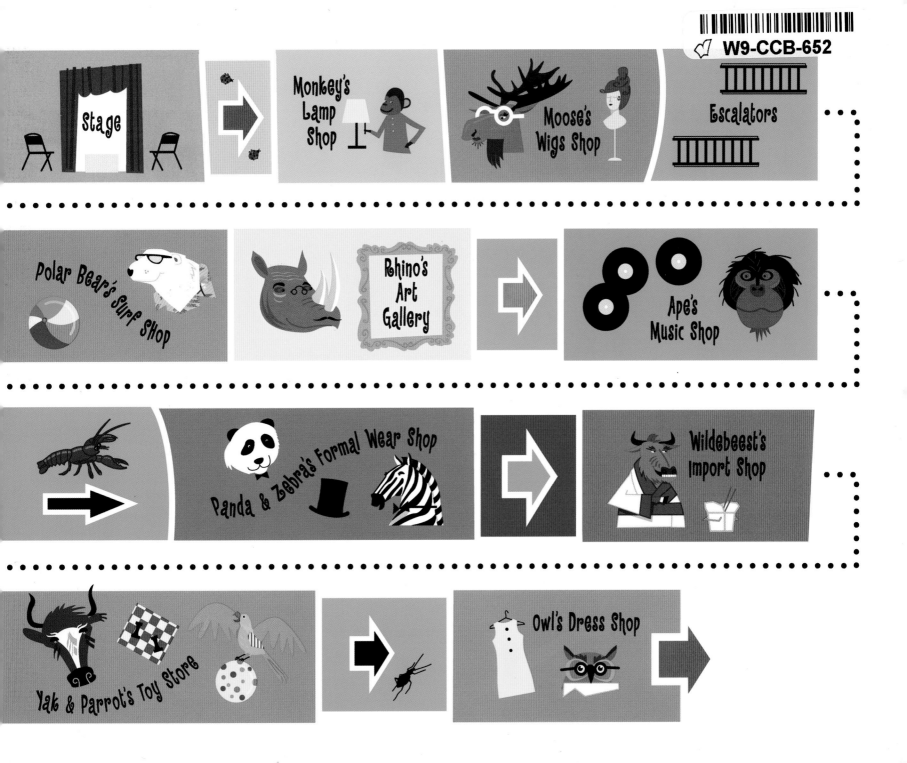

THE ANIMAL MALL

by **Cooper Edens** and **Daniel Lane**

illustrated by Edward Miller

Dial Books for Young Readers • New York

We went to the Animal Mall,
There were shops and stores for all.
The cool Baboon,
By his neon moon,
Was modeling jeans for fall.

It was then that we shouted: "Hurray!
Happy birthday, Mom! You're A-okay!
So choose something nice,
Don't think of the price!"
And Mom said, "But we've got all day!"

SALE

Right by the escalators . . .
There were eager Alligators,
Each with a balloon,
For a concert at noon,
To sell refrigerators.

Ice Cold Smoothies

There were lively Penguins so loud,
Up in a Styrofoam cloud.
All had suspenders,
And high-powered blenders
To mix smoothies for the crowd.

Upstairs at the Animal Mall,
Were shopping carts by the wall . . .
Where proud Peacocks
Sold wild argyle socks,
Crying, "One size will fit all!"

Toucan's Rare Bookstore

Next was Toucan's Rare Bookstore,
Filled up from ceiling to floor.
"First editions,
In perfect conditions!"
She squawked from a perch by the door.

We came to the pert Polar Bear,
Who with his aquatic flair . . .
Had a surf shop
That offered the top
In tropical leisure wear.

SURFSHOP

The Rhino Gallery,
Renowned for art mastery . . .
"Vintage Van Goghs,
Priceless Picassos—
And never a forgery!"

There was a family of Apes,
With racks of records and tapes . . .
And with each CD,
They would give away free
Rubber bananas and grapes.

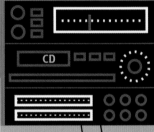

YOGURT

Al's Fridge Land

Al's Fridge Land

SALE SALE SALE

Al's Fridge Land

Al's Fridge Land

SALE SALE SALE

At the Lion's Yogurt Stand,
Right across from Al's Fridge Land . . .
We stopped to eat,
And we all tapped our feet
To the swinging Animal Band.

Al's Fridge Land

Al's Fridge Land

Al's Fridge Land

And as we enjoyed the show,

Al himself said to Mom, "Do you know,

Avocado green

For a fridge is so keen!"

But Mom smiled and shook her head no.

SALE SALE SALE

THE ANIMAL BAND

The Zebra and Panda Bear
Gave advice on formal wear . . .
"Dress up at night,
In chic black and white—
It's right for any affair!"

The wise Wildebeest,
Who hailed from the Far East . . .
Held karate sessions
And wok cooking lessons
For throwing a stir-fry feast.

At Croc's Deep Space Arcade,
Video games were played . . .
Like Zap Yo-yos,
Laser Dominos,
And Atomic Charade.

So we played nonstop till nightfall,
While Mom power-shopped the Mall . . .
From magic troll lamps
To giant Elvis stamps,
She still bought nothing at all.

The Yak and the Parrots sold toys,
Great fun for girls and boys!
The Yak liked games
That would challenge kids' brains,
While the Parrots liked lots of noise.

Oh, we went to the Animal Mall,
What shops! What stores! What a ball!
But what of Mom's gift?
Her bare cart had us miffed!
"Mom, could you find nothing at all?

"Nothing tie-dyed or paisley or plaid?"
Mom smiled. "Thank you, dear Twins and Dad.
But nowhere in sight
Was there any gift quite
As much fun as the day that we've had!"

So our little family
Went home most happily.
Mom's gift was the fun
Had by everyone
On our trip to the Animal Mall!

CLOSED

Published by Dial Books for Young Readers
A division of Penguin Putnam Inc.
345 Hudson Street
New York, New York 10014

Library of Congress Cataloging in Publication Data
Edens, Cooper.
The Animal Mall/by Cooper Edens and Daniel Lane; illustrations by Edward Miller—1st ed.
p.   cm.
Summary: Rhyming text and illustrations depict a family's adventures at the Animal Mall.
ISBN 0-8037-1984-1
[1. Shopping malls—Fiction. 2. Animals—Fiction. 3. Stories in rhyme.]
I. Lane, Daniel, date. II. Miller, Edward, ill. III. Title.
PZ8.3.E21295An 2000   [E]—DC20   96-2969   CIP AC

The illustrations in this book were created on the computer.

In memory of T-Rex
—C.E. & D.L.

To my sister, Denise
—E.M.

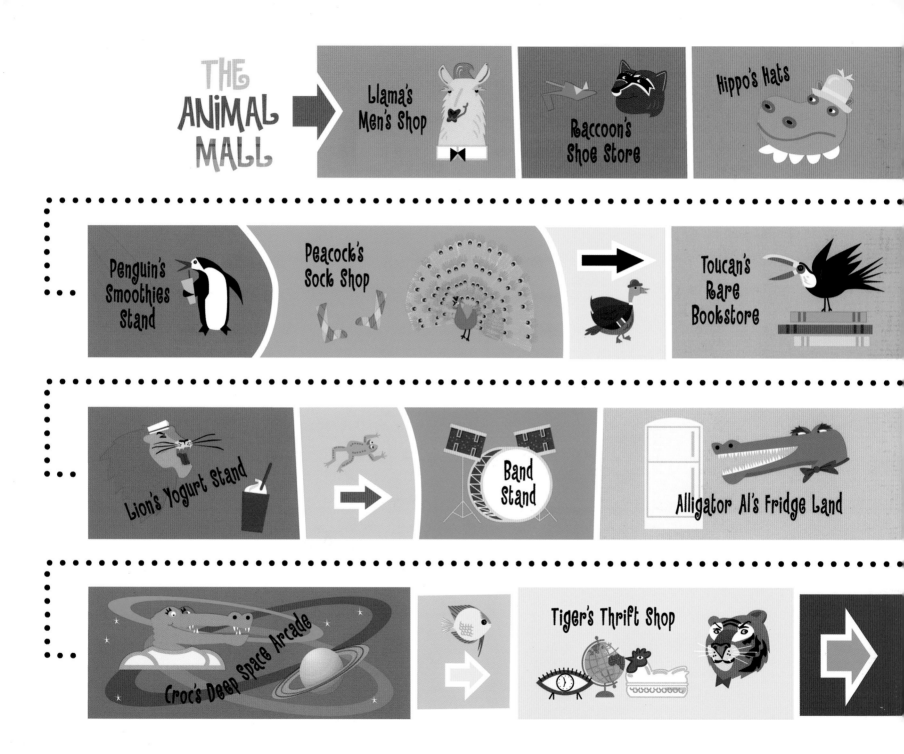